MOON SHADOWS

A SHORT STORY

KATHRYN KALEIGH

KST Publishing

MOON SHADOWS

Martin did not believe in ghosts.

But the young lady standing in the window of the vacant house across the street pulled at him.

She stood there every night.

Martin, a practical man, set out to solve a legend from 1812.

A haunting short story from best-selling author Kathryn Kaleigh.

Sign up to receive email updates

www.kathrynkaleigh.com
www.kstpublishing.com

kathryn@kstpublishing.com

Chapter 1

1812

"*I*'m afraid I have some rather disturbing news, my dear," Jonathan frowned and twisted his cigar stub until it lay cooling in a tattered lump.

Ophelia noted the change to seriousness in her betrothed's tone and turned to study his face.

"What is it?" she asked, forgetting the sampler she had been embroidering.

"Britain is refusing to cease its naval blockades and too many of our worthy seamen are being forced to serve on British ships."

He stood up and went to look out the full-length window. He stood tall and proud with his hands behind his back and his chin held high. He continued to stare and tried to put a note of courage in his voice he did not feel.

"I must go," he said.

Ophelia didn't answer. Instead, she took her time and finished the *s* on her *Home Sweet Home* sampler.

Somehow the lump in her throat took away from the little hearts and butterflies that she'd created with hundreds of tiny stitches.

Jonathan watched the approaching steamer until it glided out of sight, then turned to study his promised bride-to-be.

"Ophelia…" His voice was hoarse, even to his own ears.

She answered him then, with a calmness and determination known only to women.

"I've heard much talk of this war." She tugged too hard on the pink thread.

It snapped.

"When do you leave?"

"In the morning." Standing tall, he linked his hands behind his back.

"So soon?" Still. No emotion in her voice.

"I would have told you sooner, but I didn't want to prolong the grief."

"I could have been prepared." Her voice was soft and he heard a hint of pain.

He went to her and, kneeling in front of her, took her hands in his and looked into her eyes.

The seconds ticked slowly away. As slowly as the sluggish Ouachita River seemed to inch its way toward the Gulf of Mexico.

But like the river, their emotions were rushing and turbulent beneath the deceptive calm.

"I'm a sailor," Jonathan said softly. "My father owns ships and I sail them. My country needs me."

She kept her gaze steady on his.

"I understand Jonathan. You know I do…." She swallowed. "It's just… Our wedding was to be in two weeks."

She blinked hard, determined not to let him see her tears of despair.

"I want to be your wife."

Jonathan kissed her palms and stood up, pulling her with him. The sampler fell unnoticed to the floor as he hugged her close and held her against his chest.

"Ophelia," he said. "Will you wait for me?"

She pulled back and looked into his eyes.

All her passion for this man spilled forth to combine with his to create a web around them.

Time stood still.

"I will," she answered. "wait for you forever."

Chapter 2

Today

The wind was cold coming off the river. It was a damp chill that kept most people inside after dark. The barren oak tree limbs looked strange and misshapen in the dim moonlight.

It was the fifth night in a row since moving into the neighborhood that Martin had noticed the motionless form in the window above.

He turned around, looked behind the neighboring houses, and saw the gentle incline of the levy protecting Monroe from the Ouachita River.

Martin did not like mysteries. His world moved in a realm of black and white.

Determined to find an explanation, he went to visit a man who had lived his entire life across the street from this vacant house.

Billy Cooper.

Martin rang the doorbell again and pulled his coat tighter. He was about to leave when he heard shuffling and Billy yelling.

"I'm coming. Just a minute."

Shortly thereafter, a hefty middle-aged man opened the door and invited him in.

"Come in, Martin. Come in. It's too cold to be standing outside. What are you doing out there?" Billy slapped Martin on the shoulder as they shut out the cold.

"The wife went on up to bed," Billy continued and motioned for Martin to take a seat.

"How do you like your new house? I seen where you painted it. Looks real good." He dropped into his faded green recliner.

Martin sat on the sofa between the black cocker spaniel and an empty pizza box.

"I can't stay long, Billy. I just wanted to ask you about the old deserted house next to mine."

"Ohhh." Billy stood up . "Now there's a mystery if I ever heard one. But first I'll get you a beer."

Billy nodded in emphasis and soon returned with a beer. Martin wiped the top off with his handkerchief before he opened the can.

"Who is that girl?" Martin brought back the subject. "who stands upstairs looking out the window at night? She never moves. She just stands there. Staring."

Billy drank deeply.

"How long have you lived in the neighborhood? Three weeks?"

Martin nodded and Billy continued.

"Yes sir. You're getting broke in real fast. Say, do you get out much at night? I ain't sure that's such a good thing to do, Martin."

Martin frowned, set his beer down, and leaned forward. "I was told that old house was deserted. An old southern mansion that nobody could afford to buy and fix up. Who lives there?"

He set his beer on the coffee table littered with empty beer cans and used paper plates.

Billy set his own beer down, leaned back in the easy chair and studied a crack in the ceiling tile.

"What did you see, Buddy?"

Martin frowned again, but this was getting out of hand and he had to know.

"Like I said. The girl. She's not very old. With long hair. She stands up in the second story window."

Billy was quiet now. And very still as he listened. "Is that all?" he asked, his voice hushed.

"There's a light behind her. It must be from another room because it's like a faint glow." Martin paused, but Billy didn't respond. "Who is she?"

"Her name's said to be Ophelia."

"You don't know?" Martin was getting frustrated now.

"According to legend, her name's Ophelia."

Martin let the legend part go unnoticed for the moment.

"What is she looking at?" he asked.

"They say she's watching for Jonathan." Billy spoke softly.

"Who the hell is Jonathan?"

"Look Martin," Billy said. "It's late and I don't think you'll want to sit here while I recount an old legend that I don't think you're ready for.

Martin picked up his beer. Sipped. then he leaned back on the sofa and stretched out his long legs. He was prepared to stay until he had an answer.

"Ok, Billy. Let's have it. Out with it."

Billy sat up in his chair, then leaned back and promptly sat up again.

"Jonathan was supposed to be Ophelia's lover. They say she's waiting for him."

"Where is he?"

"He went to the war."

Martin took a deep breath. Closed his eyes for a moment, then tried to disguise a scowl which turned out to be an odd cross between a look of sickness and a smile.

"Ok," he said. "So he's off to fight in a war. Who knows what war, but a war. Why is she just waiting?"

"The story says she promised."

"Billy. Just tell me the story—or legend—or whatever it is you're talking about."

Billy looked at his watch, popped another beer can, and proceeded to tell his new neighbor the old tale he'd heard since he was a kid.

"They say Jonathan went to fight in the war of 1812." Billy ignored the quizzical look he was getting and continued.

"Jonathan and Ophelia were supposed to get married. But he had to go fight. She promised to wait for him to return."

Billy rubbed his hand over his chin. "But he never came back."

"He jilted her?" Martin asked.

"No," Billy said, his expression grim. "He died. I think maybe it was the Battle of Lake Erie up north—or something—in the fall of 1812."

Martin took another sip of beer. "So… that's interesting, but who's staying in the deserted house?"

Billy groaned and leaned forward, shaking his head. "This is why we don't tell people. I told you. Nobody. The girl is Ophelia."

"But that can't be," Martin said, setting his beer down again. He'd lost what little taste he had for it.

"She would be dead by now. Really. What is the girl doing in the house?"

"Exactly. She'd waiting. Just like she promised. When she heard that Jonathan had been killed, she locked herself in that room and died of a broken heart."

Martin ignored the chill that traveled down his spine.

"Why that room?"

"I don't know." Billy was becoming irritated now. "It appears to have the best view of the river."

"Do you believe in this legend?" Martin asked.

"It's not for me to believe or not," Billy said. "It's just a legend."

"It's ridiculous." Martin stood up and started for the door.

He stopped, turned around, and said. "I'll go there right now and prove it. There is a girl in that house. I'll go there and prove it."

As Martin headed to the door, Billy jumped up. "No!"

Martin stopped and turned around.

"No," Billy repeated, more calmly now. "I mean. You can't. It's private property. Besides that. It's locked."

"I'll break the door down just to show you there are no ghosts in that house. There are no ghosts anywhere for that matter."

"Wait a minute," Billy said. "I told you. It's only a legend."

Martin blew out a breath.

"If it's only a legend, then who is that girl?"

"Ok. Martin. Tomorrow. We'll go there tomorrow night."

Martin rubbed his chin and studied the other man. "Ok. Why not?"

"Meet me outside at Midnight." Billy's face was pale. "We'll go inside and see that nobody is there."

Chapter 3

*T*he moon was full. Martin stood beneath one of the ancient oak trees and stared up at the window of the huge antebellum house.

The girl was not there.

He stomped his feet against the chill and waited *for* Billy.

It was ten minutes after midnight when Billy joined him.

The first thing Martin realized was that Billy had the foresight to bring a flashlight.

"How do we get in?" Martin asked.

"There's a loose screen," Billy said, scanning the flashlight upward toward the windows.

"How do you know?" Martin said, scanning the many windows of the house.

"Look," Billy said. "Do you want in or not?"

"Ok. Ok. Let's go." Martin started for the front window.

Billy caught his arm and stopped him.

"No," he said. "Wait. It's in back. Besides…" He glanced toward the empty street. "I don't want anybody calling the cops on us."

"Who's going to call the police. I'm the closest neighbor and I'm here with you."

"Well, at any rate," Billy said. "I'm the one who knows how to get in. Let's use the back window."

"Ok."

But Billy didn't move.

"Are you sure you don't want to get a beer first?" he asked.

"No, Billy." Martin put his hands on his hands. "Are you afraid?"

"Are you kidding?" Billy said. "Let's go."

The two men *walked* cautiously around to the back of the house. The only sound came from their icy breath and the dry leaves crunching beneath their feet.

The screen on the bottom window to the far right slipped easily to the side. Billy pushed open the creaking window and they climbed in.

"Why do I feel like I'm breaking in on somebody?" Billy mused.

"I don't know," Martin said. "You said there was nobody in here."

"They say Ophelia's here."

Martin rolled his eyes, but didn't say anything.

The furniture was covered with white sheets, but even the dim flashlight couldn't help but reveal the cypress paneling and oak floors.

They climbed the stairs.

Martin's mouth gaped open just a little at the unexpected grandeur of the house.

"Look at that," Billy shined the flashlight on a table that had been left uncovered.

Above the table hung a faded embroidered sampler.

All the letters were there, but it didn't look quite finished.

It read *Home Sweet Home.*

A chill ran down Martin's spine.

Billy chuckled at Martin's expression of awe and the offended jerked his mouth shut and held it there.

They came to the sitting room where Ophelia supposedly waited.

They cautiously peered through the door. It was dark and quiet.

The furniture here was covered with sheets, too. There were no curtains on the windows and the barren oak branches obscured what may once have been a clear view to the river.

Martin let his breath out quietly so as to not let Billy know he'd been holding it.

They eased over to one side—away from the window—and crouched low to wait and watch.

Billy's watch beeped its half hour signal.

As they waited, it beeped again.

Billy began to fidget.

"Ok, Martin," he said. "are you satisfied? There is nobody here."

Martin cut his eyes at the other man.

"No." He shook his head. "Maybe she knows we're here and that's why she'd not showing up."

He glanced back toward the door. "Maybe we should search the house."

"You won't find nobody."

Martin scowled at him, but sat back and continued to stare at the window.

Billy checked his watch.

"What time is it?" Martin whispered.

"2:03."

"Crap. It's cold." Martin shivered.

"Shhh."

The seconds ticked past. Martin's eyes were beginning to dry out from trying not to blink. He exhaled slowly and breathed deeply.

"Let's go," he said. This was hooey.

Billy didn't answer. But he was up and out the door before Martin could stand.

They practically slid down the stairs, ran through the house, and leaped out the back window. When the window was down and the screen back in place, neither man spoke as Martin followed Billy around to the front of the house.

"Ok," Billy said. "Look Martin. Don't bother me about this again. It's a legend. Nothing more."

Billy turned on his heel and strode across the street to his house.

Martin walked halfway up his own sidewalk, but then he stopped and turned back toward the old, deserted house.

He eased up behind one of the ancient oak trees and cautiously peered around it.

The full moon outlined the house and concealed the peeling paint. His heartbeat quickened as he realized that if had he been standing in this exact spot two hundred years earlier, he would be seeing the exact think he saw at this moment.

"Why isn't she there?" he asked himself, as the clouds drifted over the moon, leaving him in darkness.

As though on impulse, Martin hurried around to the back of the house and once again removed the screen and slid the window up.

He crawled into the blackness, relying on instinct to make his way through the dark house.

It was about ten minutes later as Martin approached Ophelia's room that he felt the hair tingle on the back of his neck.

Not even the bare windows could account for all the light coming through any window other than that one.

Martin held his breath and inched ever so slowly toward the room, all the while keeping close to the wall.

At last Martin reached the door and stopped. He did not move a muscle or breathe. His heart pounded and his breath caught in his throat.

She was there.

Ophelia was there waiting for Jonathan.

Just as she had promised—so many years ago.

Chapter 4

Martin stood frozen—transfixed between fear and awe.

Then something happened.

Ophelia turned and looked at him.

Her expression was as full of surprise and fear as his was.

Only she was almost transparent. And her eyes held more knowledge than any human he'd ever seen.

Martin stared at her.

And through her.

As he watched, her expression became serene and she smiled.

Then she was gone.

He was left alone in the dark, moonlit room.

But he was no longer afraid.

And he no longer doubted that legends were there for a reason.

They all started somewhere.

Chapter 5

*M*artin never saw Ophelia again.

However, every night for the rest of his long life, Martin made it a point to walk to the old house next to his and look up the window.

He'd stand there, the seconds turning into minutes. Sometimes he'd stand there for over an hour.

Eventually, three decades later, the house sold and a family moved in.

They put up light, gossamer curtains that fluttered when the window was left open on those rare days when the weather was temperate enough that air conditioning wasn't needed.

Martin got to know them over time.

They never once suggested that their home might be haunted.

Martin never mentioned the experience to anyone, but neither did he ever again question the existence of ghosts.

KATHRYN KALEIGH

Want to be notified when Kathryn Kaleigh has a new release?
Sign up here to receive email updates:

www.kathrynkaleigh.com
www.kstpublishing.com
kathryn@kstpublishing.com

ALSO BY KATHRYN KALEIGH

HISTORICAL WESTERN ROMANCE

Finding Natalie

Promising Samantha

Falling for Allyson

Saving Savannah

Claiming Charlie

CHURNING BUTTER AND COMPANIONSHIP COLLECTION

For Churning Butter and Companionship

The Locket

Westward Bound

Westward Destiny

A Woman's Honor

Southern Hearts

Churning Butter and Companionship Collection Volume One

HISTORICAL ROMANCE

Southern Belle Civil War Collection Volume One

Southern Belle Civil War Collection Volume Two

Southern Belle Civil War Collection Volume Three

Southern Belle Civil War Collection Volume Four

Southern Belle Civil War Collection Volume Five

Southern Belle Civil War Collection Volume Six

Southern Belle Civil War Collection Volume Seven

Timeless Christmas

The Cameo

Harvest Moon

Flower Moon

Crescent Moon

Jazzy

Sapphire Seconds

The Phantom Train

Moonbeams and Time Whispers

TIME WHISPERS SERIES

Time Whispers Collection Volume One

Time Whispers Collection Volume Two

Time Whispers Mississippi River Collection

Time Whispers

Arkansas Time Whispers

Mississippi Time Whispers

Missouri Time Whispers

Tennessee Time Whispers

Louisiana Time Whispers

Illinois Time Whispers

Iowa Time Whispers

Minnesota Time Whispers

Wisconsin Time Whispers

Alabama Time Whispers

Georgia Time Whispers

South Carolina Time Whispers

CUPID'S KISS ROMANCE COLLECTION

Cupid's Kiss Collection Volume 1

Cupid's Kiss Collection Volume 2

Cupid's Kiss Collection Volume 3

Cupid's Kiss Collection Volume 4

Cupid's Arrow - Cupid's Kiss Collection Volume 5

Cupid's Kiss Collection Volume 6

Begin Again

Love Again

Falling Again

Just Happened

Just Maybe

Just Pretend

Just Because

Just Us

Just Once

Just Stay

Just Chance

Just Believe

Home for Christmas

Just One Night

Paper Airplanes

Map of the Heart

Maybe One Day

Just Christmas

In the Beginning

Miracle at Christmas

Magic of Christmas

A Chance Christmas

After Beginning Again

Snowball's Chance

ROMANTIC SUSPENSE COLLECTION

Serenity

Lost and Found

Courting Alley Cat

All I Want for Christmas

STAND ALONE

Shattered Magenta Short Story Collection

Spells and Other Useful Things

The Daffodils

Liberty Stance

Moon Shadows

The Unexpected

Finding Christmas

The Promise Point

Take the Leap

Silver Linings

Once More with Love

A Fairy Tale Christmas

Cupid Wings

Hidden

After the Summer

A Rainy Sunday Morning

A Rainy Monday Morning

A Rainy Tuesday Morning

A Rainy Wednesday Morning

A Rainy Thursday Morning

A Rainy Friday Morning

A Rainy Saturday Morning

Rainy Mornings Collection

Unbalanced Deception

Fractured

Apartment 602

Shattered Memories

Summer Love

Almost Midnight

Change of Heart

FATED MATES SEXY ROMANCE

Riley's Mate

Aiden's Mate

Brayden's Mate

KAT TALES

Kat Tales Volume One

Kat Tales Volume Two

Kat Tales Volume Three

Kat Tales Volume Four

Kat Tales Volume Five

Kat Tales Volume Six

Kat Tales Volume Seven

Kat Tales Volume Eight

Kat Tales Volume Nine

Kat Tales Volume Ten

Kat Tales Volume Eleven